To all the people who are one day forced
to put their lives in suitcases,
leave their homes, and start over again.

— M. M.

To my grandparents Tomás and Consuelo
and my great-aunts María and Enriqueta.

— E. S. G.

First published in the United States in 2022
by Eerdmans Books for Young Readers,
an imprint of Wm. B. Eerdmans Publishing Co.
Grand Rapids, Michigan

www.eerdmans.com/youngreaders

Text © 2020 Mónica Montañés
Illustrations © 2020 Eva Sánchez Gómez

Originally published in Spain as *Los distintos*
© 2020 Ediciones Ekaré, Barcelona, Spain

English-language translation © Lawrence Schimel 2022

Manufactured in the United States of America

30 29 28 27 26 25 24 23 22   1 2 3 4 5 6 7 8 9

ISBN 978-0-8028-5598-5

A catalog record of this book is available from the Library of Congress

Illustrations created with charcoal, pastel, and colored pencils

Support for the translation of this book was
provided by Acción Cultural Española, AC/E.
accioncultural.es

Eerdmans Books for Young Readers would like to thank Fulbright-National Geographic
Digital Storyteller, Destry Maria Sibley, a writer, producer, and descendant of a Spanish
Civil War refugee, for her input and assistance with this project.

The note from the publisher, endnote, glossary, and resources have been added by
Eerdmans for the readers of this English-language edition.

Different

A STORY OF THE SPANISH CIVIL WAR

WRITTEN BY **Mónica Montañés** • ILLUSTRATED BY **Eva Sánchez Gómez**

TRANSLATED BY **Lawrence Schimel**

EERDMANS BOOKS FOR YOUNG READERS

GRAND RAPIDS, MICHIGAN

A Note from the Publisher

In July 1936, a group of Spanish generals led a coup against their country's democratic government, starting the Spanish Civil War. The country was divided: some of the population supported the rebellion, but many Spaniards were still loyal to their elected leaders. Over the next three years, the two sides clashed in cities and towns across the country, with bloody consequences for both active fighters and ordinary citizens.

On April 1, 1939, the Spanish Republic fell. General Francisco Franco announced the end of the war and the start of a new authoritarian regime. Franco was now the dictator of Spain, and his far-right Falange party was now the country's only legal form of political expression. For anyone who opposed Franco's rule, Spain became a place of constant danger.

As you experience these events through the eyes of Socorro and Paco, you may encounter several unfamiliar cultural and historical figures and concepts. For help navigating this complex history, we encourage you to refer to the endnote, glossary, and further reading at the end of this book.

We are deeply grateful for the work of the author, illustrator, and translator to present this period with accuracy and sensitivity. We are honored to share this story with you.

Paco

The Man of the House

Life can change suddenly and without warning. I know because it happened to me. I was half under the bed because that was where my plane had landed. It was my favorite plane. At that moment, my only concern was to rescue it quickly before I needed to sneeze. If I sneezed, my mother would get worried and make me take a spoonful of medicine that tasted awful. There was a lot of dust under my bed, and the floor was freezing. I felt like my elbows and belly were going to freeze, too.

Just when my fingers had managed to reach the plane's wings, I heard my father's voice calling for me. I went into the living room, acting as if I were flying, with my two arms spread wide, steering clear of the furniture where I might find the enemy attacking me, imitating the sounds of my plane and the bombs it released as it passed.

I stopped short when I saw my father looking very serious, standing next to a suitcase. He called me Paco, not Paquito, which is what everyone calls me. He said that he had to leave Spain. That from this moment on, I would be the man of the house, and that I would have to take care of my mother and my sister.

I felt afraid. I wanted to cry. I was only nine years old. But I stayed silent. And I didn't cry. I couldn't. He had always told me that men don't cry, and that is what I had just become: a man.

From the window, I saw my father leave the building with his suitcase. Two Assault Guards were waiting for him in the street. It was starting to snow. I remained there, watching how my father walked along the sidewalk, until he turned the corner and I couldn't see him any more. Only then did I realize I still had the plane in my hand. I stared at it without knowing what to do with it. Only children pretended to pilot toy planes, I thought. And according to what my father had just told me, I was no longer a child.

Socorro

The Girl Who Was Never Hungry

I hated to be in the pueblo. It's not that I didn't like the village or its people. It was very pretty, and everyone loved me to pieces and treated me well. I had lived there before, because when the war started, my father took my mother, my brother Paquito, and me to live in the pueblo, where everyone is related to us. That's not an exaggeration—in almost every house there's someone who calls me cousin or niece. What's more, that's where my first tooth fell out and where I saw the underbelly of a German plane for the first time. But this time was different. This time they had left me there alone.

I wanted to be with my mother. I closed my eyes and saw her right there, beside me, like always. The day the German plane flew over us, Mama hugged Paquito and me tightly, covering us with her body, afraid a bomb would drop. But that didn't happen. The plane kept flying and, after a while, we heard a very loud sound. I didn't know what it was because I had never heard an explosion before. They didn't explain it to us—they never explained anything to us children—but I could hear the women whispering to one another that the plane had dropped a bomb on the town next to ours and many people had been killed.

That's how I understood what a war meant, and why all the adults were always so afraid. Well, not always. Sometimes they smiled because the crop had been better this year than previous years or because the rice they had just cooked had turned out delicious.

In the pueblo was also where I ate paella without a plate for the first time. We were each given a fork so we could eat directly from the pan the paella was cooked in. I liked that idea because I thought that this way, no one would realize that I wasn't eating. But I was wrong. When everyone else had finished, there was one intact portion left over, a perfect triangle of rice, right there, giving me away. It's not that I don't like rice: what I didn't like was eating. I am never hungry, and everyone always gives me a lot of grief about this.

Still, aside from the meals, and the day the German plane flew over us, I had a good time in the pueblo during the war.

But the second time I had to live in the pueblo, things were very different. And not just because I was seven years old, but because my mother had left me there all alone, with my aunts and uncles and cousins. I didn't understand it, and I was very angry. They explained to me that my father had needed to leave Spain, and that my mother couldn't keep me with her because there wasn't enough food for everyone. That excuse was absurd to me. Why, I was never hungry! So the fact that my mother couldn't feed me was another reason for me to be home with her. Paquito does eat a lot. However, they hadn't brought him to the pueblo. He had been able to remain in our house because he was a boy and not a girl like me. Everything was so unfair.

The women of the pueblo kept coming to me and saying, "Look what I baked for you, Socorritos, stop

crying and eat it, it's delicious, go on." But I didn't want food. The only thing I wanted was to be with Mama.

Paco

The Theft of a Sandwich

I was hungry, very hungry, all the time. My mother wasn't given the ration book that would let her get food because the officials knew she was the wife of a "Rojo" who had fought for the old Republic. That's why we had to rent our home out to an English family, who lived in the house as if they were the owners. And we had to settle for staying in the servant's room. My mother cleaned the house, and washed the English family's clothes and cooked for them. From what was left over, she fed me, my grandmother, and my sister Socorro, who had come back from the pueblo.

    At school, it was hard for me to concentrate. Especially during the first two hours of the morning, when the only thing I could do was think of what

Pascual, the boy who sat in front of me, would bring to eat for his merienda. He lived in the countryside and came to class by train. His mother did have the resources to feed him and every day sent him with an enormous loaf of bread filled with tortilla de patatas and with chorizos, morcillas, ham, peppers, onions . . .

The smell of those marvels went straight to my nose, torturing me. And I couldn't pay attention, not to the math teacher or the history teacher. My mind was obsessed with stealing Pascual's pataqueta bread. He left it in the compartment under his desk, beside his notebooks.

While my teachers talked about logarithms and invading kings, I worked on my plan. Just when the bell for recess rang, I would grab Pascual's sandwich and run out of class.

I would race down the hallway, go down the stairs, cross the patio, exit the school, and I wouldn't stop running until I'd reached the plaza. Only there would I stop, sit down on the last bench, and let myself feast. I would eat that bread—the good kind—bit by bit, and that tortilla and the chorizos. I couldn't remember the last time I'd been able to cat like that. I would be so happy. The only problem was that I could never again return to school.

Stealing a classmate's lunch wouldn't be such a serious thing. But they would discover that I was hungry because I was the son of a Republican who had fled Spain. That was something no one could know. That was why I couldn't simply ask Pascual to give me his lunch. Or to share a little of it with me. It would seem strange to him, and he would mention it to others.

They would start asking questions about me, about my parents. I couldn't ask him for a little bit. I would need to steal the whole thing. But I never did. I didn't dare to.

Socorro

Socorritos and Her Strategy

Paquito and I were very different from each other, and even more different from everyone else. We were the children of a Rojo. At Paco's school, nobody knew that, but boy, did they know it at mine! Mama didn't have enough money, so we had to study in the schools chosen for us by our aunt Carmen, since she was the one who paid for our education.

The nuns admitted me because they couldn't deny entrance to the niece of a person so beloved and respected as Tía Carmen, but they knew that I was the daughter of her younger brother, the one who had to flee when Franco's army won the war. They never said so to me, but they made me feel it.

Every morning, Sor Teresa went through my bag to see what I carried. I never knew what she expected to find among my notebooks and pencils, but no other girl was ever subjected to this inspection.

They placed me in first level, even though I had already passed that when I lived in the pueblo. I guess it was their way of punishing me. But that backfired for them because it turned me into the best in the class. I knew more than all my classmates. I think it made them mad for me to be so exceptional, because they had to promote me to the second level. That didn't work out for them, either, because I took it as a challenge, studied a lot, and soon was once more the best student at my level. Furious, they moved me ahead again, to third, and I studied harder than ever. I moved up three levels during the one year that I studied there.

I hated going to that school and begged Mama to change me to another. She told me she couldn't, because that was the school that Tía Carmen paid for me to attend. So I came up with a strategy. I learned all the hymns of Franco's Falange party by heart, and every afternoon I arrived home singing them at the top of my lungs. Mama was horrified when she heard me and begged me not to sing those awful words. I told her that I couldn't do anything else because that was what the nuns taught me.

My plan worked. The following year, Mama enrolled me in another school. The teachers there were also nuns, but there they treated me like all the other girls because they didn't know who my father was. I never learned how Mama managed to pay for it or how she explained the change to Tía Carmen.

Paco

The French Teacher

I was very excited to learn how to speak French.

My father had fled to France and I dreamed of joining him there someday. The idea of surprising him with the fact that I could speak French delighted me.

I arrived at school that day feeling very content, as hungry as always, but in a good mood because we would have our first French lesson. As soon as I was in the schoolyard, I started watching the group of teachers, trying to guess which of them would be the one to teach us this new subject. I imagined that it would be obvious that he came from France, that he'd be different from the rest in how he dressed and acted.

My disappointment was complete when I learned from Joaquín (a friend who usually found everything out before I did) that not only was the French teacher a Spaniard from Valencia like us, but according to what Joaquín's older brother had told him, the new teacher was also a prominent member of the Falange party. My friend had no idea what that meant for me.

I entered the classroom feeling very tense. I didn't even pay attention to Pascual's lunch. When we were already seated, the French teacher came in, said his name was Manuel Salas, and smiled at us. He pulled out a sheet with the names and surnames of all the students. He started to take roll, but before beginning, he told us that when he called out our names, we had to say the names of our fathers and their professions.

A cold sweat broke over my entire body. Every morning, before I left for school, my mother warned me that I must never speak to anyone about my father. I already knew that, but she felt she had to always remind me of the danger we could be in if anyone discovered whose son I was.

Luckily, my surname began with the letter *M*, so I had seventeen classmates ahead of me. I thought I'd have time to invent something and be able to save myself. The teacher began his interrogation: "Álvarez, Vicente! What is your father's name and profession? Arria, Juan José! What is your father's name and profession?" and so on, student after student, with him repeating the questions and my classmates answering, while I tried to think of something.

Finally, when it was already López's turn, I had an idea: I would say that my father was a railway inspector. That's what I told the teacher, thinking I was saved. I felt my heart stop when he stared at me with a look of delight. "Your father works for the railways?" he said, his smile widening. I nodded, trying not to meet his eyes so he couldn't see my fear. "How happy that makes me, Martínez," he said. Then he added, "The next time I need to make a trip, now I know who to ask a favor from, because it's very difficult to get train tickets in these times."

I failed French because I skipped so many lessons. And I never did learn to speak the language.

Socorro

The Statue of the Unknown Man

Mama was furious with me because I never drank my milk. I really tried to drink it, but that pale, thick liquid wouldn't go down my throat. Tired of fighting with me and threatening me, of explaining how important milk was for me, she went into the kitchen to wash the pots. She left me in front of the glass, telling me that I couldn't move from that spot until I had drunk the last drop.

I was ready to spend the entire day there in punishment, but my grandmother winked at me, lifted a finger to her lips to tell me to keep the secret, picked up the glass, and started to drink my milk. I couldn't believe it! I had to swallow the urge to laugh, until I saw Mama in the doorway. I started to apologize, terrified, but Mama's anger was aimed at my abuela. It was inconceivable to her that Abuela had drunk the milk that she bought for her children at such great sacrifice. Abuela was very ashamed. She looked down and, in a whisper, confessed that she had done it because she couldn't resist the temptation. Luckily, Paquito broke the tension of that moment, shouting for us to come.

My brother, taking advantage of the fact that the English family were not in the house, had gone out onto the balcony to play. He wanted us to look at something that seemed very strange to him. A Falange truck had arrived, and several men climbed out carrying picks and shovels. Armed with these tools, they began to strike the statue that had always been in the plaza. They knocked it over, lifted it into the truck, and took it away. None of us understood this. What's more, we didn't even know who the statue was of. We had never bothered to look.

My mother couldn't resist the urge to satisfy her curiosity and went down to read the plaque that remained on the marble base, to discover the identity of this hero who so angered the Falangists. She came back quickly. It was a man named Simón Bolívar, who neither she nor we had ever heard of. Abuela dared to speak, even though her daughter was still angry with her. She told us he was the liberator of the Americas. My grandmother was very different from all the other women I knew. She didn't clean, cook, or sew. She spent the day reading books and knew lots of facts, the kind where one never knows exactly how useful they'll be in the future.

Paco

The Fifth Letter

At night, before going to bed, we listened to the news on the radio. We had to turn the volume very low so as not to bother the English tenants. The Second World War had broken out, and we hoped that the Allies would win. We thought that maybe if that happened,

they would overthrow Franco as well, and the Republic would return to Spain—and with it, my father.

That wasn't how things happened. The Allies did win, but for us everything remained the same. I stopped listening to the radio. Everything seemed very unfair to me, but there was nothing that I could do about it. I tried as hard as I could not to draw attention to myself at school. And I only hoped that a letter from my father might arrive someday, telling us that he had managed to arrange a way to get us out of that nightmare, and that we could be reunited with him.

I guess it wasn't easy to send letters to us, or perhaps some got lost along the way, because we received very few letters from my father. When I say very few, I am not exaggerating. I don't know quite what word to use to describe it—only five letters in eight long years. They were few, so very few, especially from someone whom you miss so terribly. The first two arrived from France. Then, another two came from Mexico.

The fifth letter was the most marvelous and strange of them all. Marvelous, because Father told us that he had a job and had managed to get the papers that would give us permission to leave Spain and travel to join him. Strange, because of the country where he was waiting for us. Father was no longer in Mexico, as we had thought, but in a country called Venezuela, which we had never heard of before. I had to run and find a map to see where it was.

My mother, Socorritos, and I were all stunned. That was when Abuela reminded us of the statue in the plaza that the Falangists had knocked down. She told us that Simón Bolívar was Venezuelan. Delighted,

my mother smiled and went out to the balcony again, looking at the plaza and thinking of the journey to that unknown country where, according to her, things would no doubt go very well for us.

Socorro

A Family of Strangers

It wasn't easy to reach Venezuela. Not easy at all, and very emotional. We had to take several trains to get from Valencia to the port of Cádiz. Paquito and I had never boarded a train, and we spent the entire journey glued to the window. At the port, we boarded an immense ship. It wasn't meant for passengers, so Mama, Abuela, and I settled into an improvised cabin where all us women traveling across the Atlantic would sleep; Paquito would sleep in the other berth with the men. We spent the entire day on the deck, staring at that vast quantity of water they called the ocean, which looked like it would never end. We were fascinated because, of course, it was also the first time we had ever traveled by boat.

A lot of time passed until we arrived in Cuba—and then came the best part, because we got to ride in an airplane. We had never even dreamed that one day we might travel in a real plane and fly through the air. The fear we felt when that gigantic and heavy machine began to rise toward the sky was tremendous. We couldn't believe that metal object could detach itself from the ground with us inside it. We swore that at any moment it would fall and we would sink forever into the Caribbean Sea.

   After a while, which seemed like a century to us, we heard the voice of the pilot announcing that in a few minutes we would land. On the runway, we saw that there were lots of people awaiting the passengers from our flight.

   My brother and I had our faces pressed to the window, trying to tell which of those people was my father. I couldn't see him, nor could Mama, but Paquito recognized him right away. "There he is!" he shouted. "He's the one with the black beret!" I looked where he was pointing and thought he had to be mistaken. The truth is that I didn't remember my father. He had left Spain when I was seven, and I arrived in Venezuela when I was fifteen. I confess that I had imagined he would be a tall, strong man, almost a superhero. The man my brother pointed at was thin, gangly, and had completely white hair.

We disembarked from the plane and walked toward where the man (who was in fact my father) waited for us. He seemed to stare at us in the same fearful way that we were staring at him. Which was no surprise. So many things had happened in the eight years since we last saw one another. It had also been difficult for him to recognize us, at least my brother and me. Finally he smiled and embraced us. It wasn't easy, but we had traveled halfway around the world to join him, and he had stayed alive just so he could see us again. And so, despite all of us now being so different, we hugged each other under the bright sun of that new country.

Paco

A Tickle on the Tongue

Happiness tastes like bread and butter. I didn't know that. I had never eaten butter before. I tried it for the first time when I arrived in Venezuela. It was also the first time I had ever eaten in a restaurant.

My parents talked without stopping, enjoying being able to speak together at last without worrying who might overhear.

I listened to them and ate, fascinated, spreading butter on the slices of bread that the waiter kept bringing us, as if there was an unending supply of bread in this country. For me, since I was always hungry, it was like being in paradise. And not just for me.

All of us, even Socorritos who hardly ever ate, stuffed ourselves until we were fit to burst. My father made us try the lechosa, a fruit he loved that we had never even seen. It was a little strange to us, but he didn't let us complain.

The truth is, we had nothing to complain about. We lived in wonder. We couldn't believe that there were so many trees and birds in a thousand colors all around us. That mangoes fell from trees in the middle of the street, and anyone could take them because they didn't belong to anyone. Or more accurately, the mangoes belonged to anyone who wanted to pick one and eat it. We giggled at how the Venezuelans spoke as if they were whistling, making no difference between the letters *C* and *Z*. And they never turned off the lights, as if the electricity there were free.

We couldn't believe that Caracas was lit up all the time. And the sodas! We hadn't known these sweet, multicolored drinks that tickled your tongue with their bubbles had been invented. For my family, it was a fiesta when, at six p.m., someone arrived at the pensión boarding house where we lived, carrying a lot of green, red, brown, purple, and orangish bottles, and we all sat down to drink them and talk.

Little by little, we adapted to living in Venezuela and to being foreigners. We were still different from everyone else, and that was noticeable in our accents. But at least being different had stopped being something dangerous for us.

More about Socorro and Paco's World

Spain at war with itself

On July 17, 1936, a group of Spanish military officers started the Spanish Civil War by rebelling against their country's democratically elected government, known as the "Second Republic." From the founding of the Spanish Republic in 1931, Spain's elected leaders had pushed for major social and political changes, such as limiting the power of the Roman Catholic Church and extending rights for women and minority language speakers. The rebels—the "Nationalists"—hated these new policies and longed for the country to be ruled by kings, priests, and the military. Their supporters, including aristocrats, landowners, fascist political parties, and militant Catholics, agreed that the democratic government had been a poor replacement for the majestic Spanish Empire. With their coup, the Nationalists hoped to overthrow the Republic and rule Spain in traditional, imperial ways once again.

Commanded by Francisco Franco and other rebel generals, the Nationalist army marched across Spain, trying to bring all of Spain under its rule. But the Republican government still controlled much of the country (including its capital, Madrid), and their supporters—the "Republicans"—would not surrender quietly. Republican fighters and supporters included a wide and often conflicting range of progressive activists, including students, liberals, socialists, communists, anarchists, and labor organizers. As the war progressed, these differences would cause constant infighting on the Republican side and weaken its efforts to unite against the Nationalists.

The world's response

As news of the Spanish Civil War spread, people across the world responded with shock and horror. Many had thought World War I (1914–1918) had been the "war to end all wars," but—less than two decades later—the Spanish Civil War was threatening to split the globe into sides once again. Explanations abounded for the tensions in Spain, and rampant propaganda (a frequently political, often misleading form of communication) only deepened the gaps between Nationalists, Republicans, and those who supported them.

Across the world, onlookers worried that Spain's war could be the first battle of a second world war. Hoping to stop the violence from spreading, most countries decided not to participate in the fighting. By August 1936, France, Britain, Italy, Germany, and the Soviet Union had all signed a nonintervention agreement, promising not to get involved in Spain. Though United States President Franklin Roosevelt sympathized with the Republican cause, the US Congress

passed a series of Neutrality Acts and banned arms sales to
both Nationalists and Republicans.

But all these promises could not and did not stop
outside forces from participating in Spain's war. Even while
Italy and Germany publicly signed neutrality agreements, the
two countries—ruled by fascist dictators Benito Mussolini
and Adolf Hitler—sent thousands of troops, weapons,
and aircraft to the Nationalist rebels. The Soviet Union—
ruled by communist dictator Joseph Stalin—sent arms
and funds to the Republicans, also ignoring its previous
promises of neutrality. Though, like the United States, most
democratic governments remained officially neutral, many
of their citizens openly declared their loyalties. Around
35,000–40,000 volunteers from over 50 countries (including
the United States, Chile, and Ireland) joined "international
brigades" and traveled to Spain to help the Republicans.

Bombs over Spain

Over the next three years of conflict, children like Socorro
and Paco would learn to recognize the horrible sound of
planes overhead. The Spanish Civil War was the first conflict
in which an army deliberately targeted civilians with
bombs as part of their military strategy. Hoping to force a
Republican surrender, the Nationalists bombed both army
encampments and civilian towns. The Nationalists' German

and Italian allies willingly supplied the means for these attacks, using Spain as a testing ground for their own military tactics and weaponry. Those on the ground never knew where the next bomb would land, or what it might destroy.

One young Spaniard, Rafael Morante, was only five years old when he survived the German bombing of Almería. Rafael's family had arrived in the town for a seaside vacation, but they found themselves in the midst of a Nazi counterattack. In a 2000 interview recorded in the book *They Still Draw Pictures*, Rafael remembered running hand-in-hand with his mother while bombs exploded around them: "I thought the world had come to an end, and would never be the same again."

On April 26, 1937, one of the war's most deadly days, German and Italian aircraft bombed the town of Guernica, killing and wounding hundreds of civilians—a third of the town's population—in only a few violent hours. When news of the tragedy in Guernica reached the painter Pablo Picasso, he began to create *Guernica*, an image of war's impact on human lives. When the painting was displayed at the 1937 World's Fair, it raised international awareness of Spain's suffering and gathered support for the Republican cause. *Guernica* is now viewed as one of history's most influential anti-war paintings, standing as an iconic tribute to the lives threatened both back then and around the world today.

The end of the war and a new Spain

As the Spanish Civil War dragged on into 1939, hunger and military losses eroded the hopes of the Republicans and their supporters. Food shortages were constant, and the Nationalist forces were conquering city after city. On February 1, the Republican stronghold of Catalonia fell, and on March 27, the Nationalists forced the Republican air force and army to surrender Madrid. Just four days later, on April 1, 1939, Francisco Franco declared the Spanish Civil War over. Since the beginning of the war, about 500,000 people had lost their lives.

The Republic was gone, and Franco was now "El Caudillo" and "El Generalísimo"—the leader and supreme general of an authoritarian regime that would last for almost forty years. The regime carefully controlled and censored all media reports, repressing all opposing views. Franco's fascist party, the Falange, hated any hint of difference and violently persecuted "delinquents" who did not match their vision of Spain. Republican sympathizers were executed, forced into labor camps, or deported to German concentration camps. For anyone who was different, secrets became a way of life. Escape became many families' only chance of safety.

Wartime refugees

During the war, many Republican families had decided to evacuate their children, sending them away to safer countries like Mexico and England. But Franco's victory meant that few of those children ever saw their parents again. Even if the evacuees managed to return, they discovered that their families—and their country—had drastically changed since they left.

As the war progressed, and the Nationalists conquered more and more of Spain, a steady stream of refugees fled the country, hoping to find better lives beyond the bombings. Many countries were reluctant to accept Spanish refugees, and foreign governments' treatment of new arrivals varied widely. Still, after the fall of Catalonia, over 475,000 refugees crossed the border into France over a matter of weeks, terrified of violence or repression in Spain.

In February 1939, Franco closed the border with France. A lack of ships prevented many refugees from fleeing from Mediterranean ports. Escape was even more difficult than before. Those still in Spain—like Paco, Socorro, and their mother—were trapped in a new and dangerous country.

Spain beyond the wars

In September 1939, only a few months after the end of the Spanish Civil War, the long-feared Second World War began. Still reeling from its own war, Spain decided to stay officially neutral during WWII, though Franco did provide some support for the fascist Axis Powers. When Nazi Germany and Fascist Italy fell in 1945, many former Republicans hoped for a new dawn of democracy in Spain. But as the world entered a new Cold War between East and West, Fascist Spain did not truly belong to either side. Under Franco, Spain was not a capitalist democracy like the United States, and it was not a communist dictatorship like the Soviet Union. Many Western countries—including the United States—formed uneasy alliances with Spain, hoping to defeat the Soviet Union with Spanish help. Over the decades, some of the restrictive policies of Franco's regime were lifted, but Spain would have to wait until 1975—the year of Franco's death—for the dictatorship to end.

A new life beyond Spain

Even if a family or individual managed to escape Spain during the war or the dictatorship, they faced impossible choice after impossible choice. World War II only multiplied the global number of refugees, and the refugees received all kinds of responses from their new neighbors, from warm and supportive to negligent and abusive. Anti-Spanish sentiment appeared everywhere from France to Spain's former colonies in Latin America. Some argued that the newcomers would take jobs and resources from native citizens; some focused on news reports of anti-Catholic violence; some wondered why they should welcome the descendants of their oppressors. Others organized welcoming committees and financially supported Spanish refugees' transition to a new life. But no resettlement process was easy, and no refugee could predict what future awaited them outside Spain.

After fleeing to France, many Spanish exiles found themselves fighting against fascism once again. While Nazi Germany occupied France in WWII, many Spanish exiles joined resistance movements, fighting against the same country that had bombed their homeland. Other Spanish refugees, who had been placed in French internment camps when they arrived, were tragically deported to German concentration camps.

Like Paco and Socorro's family, other Spanish refugees resettled in Venezuela, Mexico, Argentina, Chile, and many Latin American countries, and began the long, hard work of building a new life in an unfamiliar place. Children grew up, found jobs, and often started families of their own. Many Spanish exiles embraced the freedoms of their new homes, starting universities, libraries, dance companies, and other cultural institutions. But they never forgot their lives in Valencia or Catalonia or the Basque country, often organizing ways to teach their children the culture and traditions of the home they had been forced to leave behind.

The legacy of the past

When Francisco Franco died on November 20, 1975, democracy could finally return to Spain. Franco named King Juan Carlos I as his successor. But rather than follow in Franco's footsteps, Juan Carlos helped modernize the country and restore the freedoms of its people. Today Spain is a parliamentary constitutional monarchy, grappling with a history of over five decades of violence and secrecy. In 2008, Spain passed "the grandchildren's law," offering citizenship to the descendants of refugees of the Spanish Civil War and Franco's dictatorship. The law allowed people from across the world to call Spain home, decades after their parents and grandparents had been forced to leave.

The lives of refugees today

For millions of people today, Paco and Socorro's experiences are not far from their own. In the years since the Spanish Civil War, violent civil wars have torn apart Syria, Sudan, and many other countries. In the years since Franco's death, dozens of dictators have seized power, oppressing all those they declare different. While millions fled Spain from the 1930s through the 1970s, those numbers are small compared to those seeking refuge across the world today. According to the United Nations High Commissioner for Refugees (UNHCR), about 84 million people were forcibly displaced from their homelands in 2021. Like Paco, Socorro, and their parents, these refugees are searching for a life of safety and dignity. Somewhere, they hope, they can finally find a home where they can be different without fear.

A Glossary of Socorro and Paco's World

abuela: Grandmother.

Assault Guards: The special police force of the Spanish Second Republic, which focused on urban and political violence. During the Spanish Civil War, most Assault Guards stayed loyal to the Republican government and defended their cities against Nationalist attacks.

Caracas: The capital and largest city of Venezuela, located in a mountain valley close to the Caribbean Sea. After the end of WWII, Venezuela hosted thousands of Spanish, Portuguese, and other European refugees, with many settling in Caracas.

chorizos: Aged Spanish pork sausages, often sliced and eaten similarly to an Italian salami.

Falange / Falangists: The far-right political party of Spain's dictator Francisco Franco, and its supporters. During the war, these people were often called "Nationalists." Franco's regime banned all opposing political parties, so many Falangists simply referred to their party as "the Movement" from 1939–1975. The party endorsed traditional beliefs and the rule of an authoritarian leader, and it was opposed to all influences of democracy, liberalism, and communism.

fiesta: Party.

Francisco Franco: A member of the military rebellion that started the Spanish Civil War, Franco rose to higher and higher prominence throughout the conflict. After the Nationalist victory in 1939, Franco became the dictator of Spain and began an authoritarian regime that would last until his death in 1975.

lechosa: A South American name for the papaya.

merienda: A small meal or snack eaten in Spain and a number of other countries between lunchtime and dinnertime.

morcillas: Seasoned Spanish blood sausages, which are cooked before eating.

paella: A beloved Spanish rice dish, originally from Valencia and considered a symbol for the region. It is traditionally cooked in a special frying pan over an open fire.

pataqueta: A traditional Valencian bread with a crusty outside and crumbly inside, made in the shape of a crescent moon.

pensión house: A guest house or boarding house, which often offers breakfast, lunch, and dinner to its lodgers, as well as housing.

pueblo: A rural town or village.

Republic: The democratic, representative government of Spain (called "The Second Republic," since an earlier Spanish attempt at democracy had failed), founded in 1931. After the deposition of King Alfonso XIII, Spaniards elected new leaders and began reforming the country's laws and institutions. In 1936, a group of dissatisfied military generals rebelled against the Republic, beginning the Spanish Civil War. The government officially surrendered to the Nationalists in 1939 after the fall of Madrid.

Republicans: Those who fought for the Spanish Republic, or those who simply supported the idea of Spanish democracy. Republicans could be communists, socialists, or democrats, and they came from a wide range of political, economic, and social backgrounds.

Rojo: "Red" in Spanish, a derogatory term used to refer to supporters of the Republican side in the Spanish Civil War. Because of communism's association with the color red, and because some—though not all—Republican supporters were communist sympathizers, their opponents often referred to them as "Reds" or "Rojos."

Simón Bolívar: A Venezuelan soldier and politician who led present-day Venezuela, Peru, Bolivia, Colombia, Ecuador, and Panama to independence from the Spanish Empire. To many Falangists, who idolized Spain's imperial past, Bolívar's revolution represented Spain's tragic decline in global power. To others, who had hated Spain's controlling influence in Latin America, Bolívar's revolution represented a joyous victory for freedom.

tortilla de patatas: Traditional Spanish potato-and-egg omelets. They can be served warm, cold, or at room temperature.

Sor: Shortened form of *soror* (sister), used with a name (*Sor Teresa*) to address Catholic sisters or nuns.

tía: Aunt.

Valencia: A Spanish city on the coast of the Mediterranean Sea, and the third-largest city in Spain (behind Madrid and Barcelona) in both the 1930s and today. During the Spanish Civil War, Valencia was bombed 442 times, leaving thousands dead and hundreds wounded. The city also served as the temporary capital of Republican Spain from November 1936 to October 1937. After the Nationalists' victory, Franco's regime banned the teaching of the regional Valencian language, a dialect of Catalan. Today Valencian schools are required to teach Catalan alongside Spanish, and all new street signs must be in Catalan.

Resources for Children & Young Adults

Aronson, Marc, and Marina Budhos. *Eyes of the World: Robert Capa, Gerda Taro, and the Invention of Modern Photojournalism*. New York: Henry Holt Books for Young Readers, 2017. Young adult nonfiction.

Ferrada, María José. *Mexique: A Refugee Story from the Spanish Civil War*. Illus. Ana Penyas. Grand Rapids, MI: Eerdmans, 2020. Picture book.

Griffiths, Katie. *The Spanish Civil War*. New York: Cavendish Square, 2018. Young adult nonfiction.

Morpurgo, Michael. *Toro! Toro!*. Illus. Michael Foreman. New York: HarperCollins, 2007. Middle grade fiction.

Robeson, Susan. *Grandpa Stops a War: A Paul Robeson Story*. Illus. Rod Brown. New York: Triangle Square, 2019. Picture book nonfiction.

Sepetys, Ruta. *The Fountains of Silence*. New York: Philomel, 2019. Young adult fiction.

Syson, Lydia. *A World Between Us*. London: Hot Key, 2012. Young adult fiction.

Resources for Older Readers

Biblioteca Virtual Miguel de Cervantes. "Los trasterrados." Spanish-language video, 4:19. October 2, 2017. cervantesvirtual.com/portales/ fundacion_pablo_ iglesias/847644_los_transterrados/. Online documentary.

Geist, Anthony L., and Peter N. Carroll. *They Still Draw Pictures: Children's Art in Wartime from the Spanish Civil War to Kosovo*. Urbana: University of Illinois Press, 2002. Adult nonfiction.

Graham, Helen. *The Spanish Civil War: A Very Short Introduction*. Oxford: Oxford University Press, 2005. Adult nonfiction.

Legarreta, Dorothy. *The Guernica Generation: Basque Refugee Children of the Spanish Civil War*. Reno, NV: University of Nevada Press, 1985. Adult nonfiction.

Museo Nacional Centro de Arte Reina Sofia. "Rethinking Guernica." https://guernica.museoreinasofia.es/en. Website.

Richards, Matt. *To Say Goodbye*. 2012. Animated film.

Sibley, Destry Maria. "Los Niños de Morelia: The Children of Morelia." ninosdemorelia.com. Website and podcast links.

Tremlett, Giles. *Ghosts of Spain: Travels Through Spain and Its Silent Past*. New York: Bloomsbury, 2008. Adult nonfiction.

The United Nations High Commissioner for Refugees (UNHCR). "Refugee Data Finder." https://www.unhcr.org/refugee-statistics/. Website.

United States Holocaust Memorial Museum. "Spanish Civil War." https://encyclopedia.ushmm.org/content/en/article/spanish-civil-war. Website.

Mónica Montañés is a Venezuelan journalist, playwright, screenwriter, and author. The original Spanish edition of *Different* was selected as a 2021 NYPL Best Spanish-Language Book and included in the White Ravens catalog. The book is based on the stories that her father José and her aunt Amparo told her about their childhood during the civil war and post-war period in Spain, and the events that caused them to leave their country to be reunited with their father, whom they had not seen for eight long years.

As an adult, Mónica moved from Caracas to Madrid with her two children, making her grandmother's journey in reverse. *Different* is her English-language debut. Follow Mónica on Instagram @monicamontanesc.

Eva Sánchez Gómez is an award-winning artist and illustrator whose other books include *The Magician's Visit* (Green Bean). She studied fine arts at the University of Barcelona, then earned an MA in illustration at the University of Valencia.

For *Different*, Eva drew from period photos and her family's stories about the era. The project brought back memories of her childhood in Puigcerdà, playing along the invisible, imperceptible-to-children "border" between Spain and France. She and her brother would set one foot on each side of the border line, always aware that each side was part of the same world. Eva lives in Spain. Visit her website at evasanchez.cat or follow her on Instagram @eva_illustration.

Lawrence Schimel is an author, anthologist, and translator of many books in both Spanish and English, including *Early One Morning* (Orca), *Niños*, and *One Million Oysters on Top of the Mountain* (both Eerdmans). His works have received many awards, including the SCBWI Crystal Kite Award, a PEN Translates Award, and the GLLI Translated YA Book Prize Honor. Lawrence lives in Madrid, Spain. Follow him on Twitter @lawrenceschimel.